This book belongs to ★

....

....

....

the Topsy-Turvies

Story by Francesca Simon
Pictures by Keren Ludlow

Dolphin

For Miranda Richardson,
with love *F.S.*

For Hannah May *K.L.*

Published as a Dolphin paperback in 1997
First published in Great Britain in 1995
by Orion Children's Books
a division of the Orion Publishing Group Ltd
Orion House
5 Upper St Martin's Lane
London WC2H 9EA

A catalogue record for this book is available from
the British Library

Printed in Italy
ISBN 1 85881 332 8

Once upon a time there lived a family called the Topsy-Turvies.

The Topsy-Turvies always got up at midnight.

They put on their pyjamas, then went upstairs and had dinner.

"Eat up, Minx," said Mr Topsy-Turvy.

Minx juggled with the sausages.

"Clever girl!" said Mr Topsy-Turvy.

"Jinx, stop eating with your fork," said Mrs Topsy-Turvy. "You know that's for combing your hair. Please use your fingers and toes."

"Could you pass the jam please, Minx?" said Mr Topsy-Turvy.
Minx dipped her fingers in the jar and hurled the jam at her father.
"Thanks," said Mr Topsy-Turvy.

"Could you pass the whipped cream please, Jinx?" said Mrs
Topsy-Turvy. Jinx flung a handful of cream at his mother.
"Thanks, dear," said Mrs Topsy-Turvy.

Then it was time for school.

After school they went to the park.

Then they played beautiful music together

and watched TV.

Afterwards they ate breakfast, then it was bathtime, and then they all went to bed.

Every night and day at the Topsy-Turvies was exactly the same, until...

one afternoon a loud knocking
at the door woke them up.

"Who could that be at this time of
day?" yawned Mrs Topsy-Turvy.

It was their neighbour, Mrs Plum.

"Oh dear," said Mrs Plum. "Were you just leaving?"

"No," said Mrs Topsy-Turvy. "Why would I go outside
wearing my coat?"

"I'm sorry to bother you," said Mrs Plum. "But I have
to go out. Could you come over and look after little Lucy?
She's as good as gold."

Mrs Topsy-Turvy was very sleepy, but she liked helping others. "Of course," said Mrs Topsy-Turvy. "We'll be undressed in a minute."

As soon as everyone was ready, they went next door to Mrs Plum's house.

"Thank you so much," said Mrs Plum. "Do make yourselves at home and have something to eat." And off she went.

"Mum, why is Mrs Plum wearing clothes *outside*?" said Minx.

"Shh," said Mrs Topsy-Turvy. "Everyone's different."

The Topsy-Turvies goggled at Mrs Plum's house. Nothing looked right.

"Poor Mrs Plum," said Mrs Topsy-Turvy. "Let's make the house lovely for her."

The Topsy-Turvies went to work.
They fixed, they fussed, and they put the room in apple-pie order.

"That's better," said Mr Topsy-Turvy.

"Careful, Lucy, don't put that apron on, you'll get
paint all over it," said Mr Topsy-Turvy.

"Lucy! Don't draw on the paper!" said Mrs
Topsy-Turvy. "Draw on the walls!"
"Isn't she naughty," said Minx.

"Not everyone can be as well behaved as you, dear,"
said Mrs Topsy-Turvy. "Lucy, what a lovely picture!"

"I'm hungry," said Jinx.

"So am I," said Minx.

Mrs Topsy-Turvy looked at the clock. It was already five.

"We might as well have breakfast," said Mrs Topsy-Turvy.

"Let's see what food we can find in the bedroom."

It took them a very long time
to find where Mrs Plum
kept her food.

"What an odd house,"
said Mr Topsy-Turvy.

"How funny to eat in the kitchen," said Minx.
"Breakfast is under the table," said Mrs Topsy-Turvy.
"Don't forget to wash your feet."

"Everything's fine," said Mr Topsy-Turvy.

"You chased away a burglar!" said Mrs Plum.
"Thank you so much. Goodness what a mess he made!"
"What mess?" said Mrs Topsy-Turvy.

The Topsy-Turvies waved goodbye and went home.

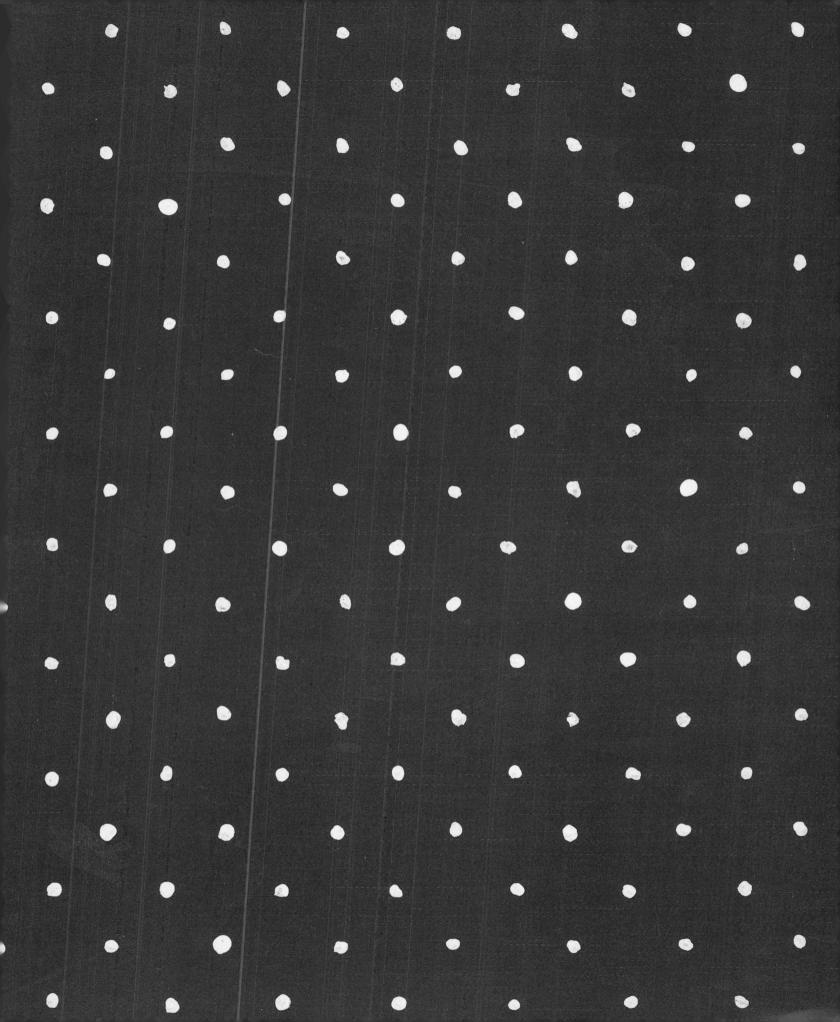